LIGHT☆BEARS™ : Answering The Call

Illustrated by Prue Berthon

Written by Fritz and Angel

This book belongs to:

Hello Dove. I've got
no-one to play with.

Come outside Fritz.
You'll find lots of
friends there.

FRITZ

You see . . .
There they all are.

But... what I really want is
someone to play with —
full time!

Meanwhile . . .
Angel is at a friend's birthday party.

Oh, it's all so beautiful...
and wonderful ...

How I wish
I could share it all
with just one special friend.

Oh dear . . . .
    Let's go and help
        Fritz and Angel.

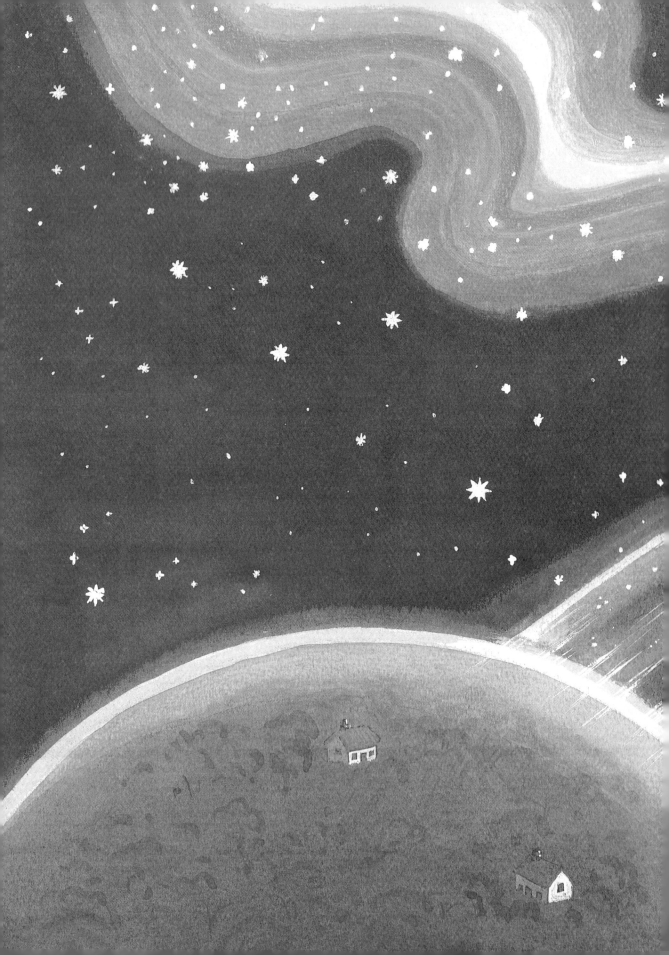

Hello Angel,
I'm your Light☆Bear.
I've come to help.

Hello Fritz.
I'm your Light☆Bear
and I've come to help.

Oh, this looks like a very special letter, doesn't it?

Hi, Angel. Please light this little candle
from that big one over there,
just like the other bears are doing.

you are my very special ☆ friend

Universal Movers

From Here . . .
. . . To There
and
. . . Everywhere

34

Thank you   Thank you
Light☆Bears.

We're so happy.

P.O Box 2800 · Santa Fe · New Mexico 87504-2800 · U.S.A

Dear Friends:

Thank you for reading our book.

We hope you liked it – and will follow our experiences and adventures to come.

If you would like more information about the Light ✷ Bears and their ideas, or details about our other books and postcards, please write to us.

We do love to hear from all our friends.

Love,

Fritz & Angel ✷

38